Groundwood Books / House of Anansi Press
110 Spadina Avenue, Suite 801, Toronto, Ontario M5V 2K4
or c/o Publishers Group West
1700 Fourth Street, Berkeley, CA 94710

We acknowledge for their financial support of our publishing program
the Canada Council for the Arts, the Government of Canada through
the Canada Book Fund (CBF) and the Ontario Arts Council.

Library and Archives Canada Cataloguing in Publication
Gay, Marie-Louise
Caramba and Henry / Marie-Louise Gay.
ISBN 978-1-55498-097-0
I. Title.
PS8563.A868C38 2011   jC813'.54   C2011-900510-7

The art was created in watercolor, pencil,
pastel and acrylic paint.
Printed and bound in China

To everyone who has seen

a flying cat or two…

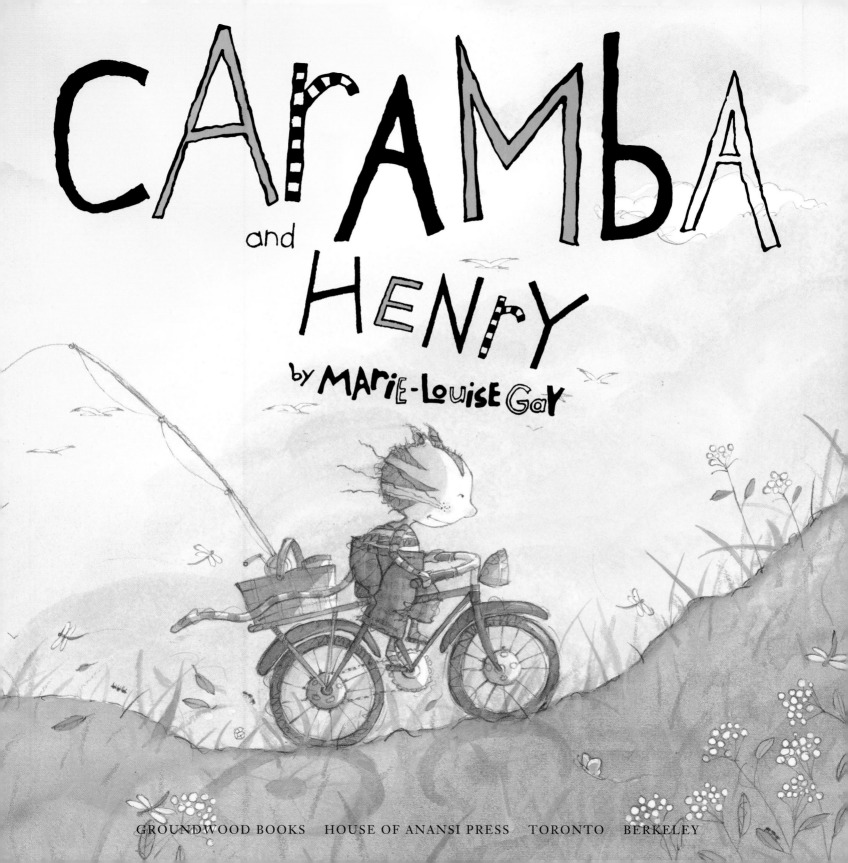

CARAMBA
and
HENrY

by MARiE-LouiSE Gay

GROUNDWOOD BOOKS   HOUSE OF ANANSI PRESS   TORONTO   BERKELEY

Caramba had always wished for a brother.
A brother he could go fishing with.
A brother to collect caterpillars with.

A brother who would love his cheese omelets.
A brother who would share all his secrets.
But Caramba had never imagined a brother like Henry.

Henry wouldn't share *anything*.

He squished Caramba's favorite caterpillars.

He threw Caramba's cheese omelets out the window.

Henry didn't talk. He yelled. Or howled. Or screamed. *All* the time.

Caramba had to wear earplugs.

"You could teach him to purr," said Portia. "You purr really well."

"Cats purr when they're happy," said Caramba. "Henry is never happy."

"And now," said Caramba, "Henry is starting to fly…"
Uh-oh, thought Portia. She knew what that meant to Caramba.
He was the only cat in the world who couldn't fly.

"I thought he would be like me," said Caramba. "I wanted to teach him to swim."

"You still can," said Portia.

"No," grumbled Caramba. "Why would he want to swim if he can fly?"

Henry was learning to fly, but he wasn't very good at it yet.
One day Henry sneezed so hard that he shot up into the air
and almost landed on Caramba's pet cactus.
But he flapped his tiny arms,
sailed upside down out the window
and fell headfirst into the duck pond.
By the time Caramba fished him out,
Henry was covered in duck feathers
and screeching like a fire alarm.

"Caramba!" said his mother. "I want you to keep an eye on Henry until he learns to fly properly."

"Me?" said Caramba. "Why me?"

"You're his big brother," answered his mother. "That's what big brothers do."

"But he won't listen to me," said Caramba. "And he screams all the time."

"I noticed," said his mother.

"Did you notice I can't fly?" said Caramba. "How can I keep up with him?"

"You are a very clever cat, Caramba," said his mother. "I am sure you'll find a way."

Caramba sighed.

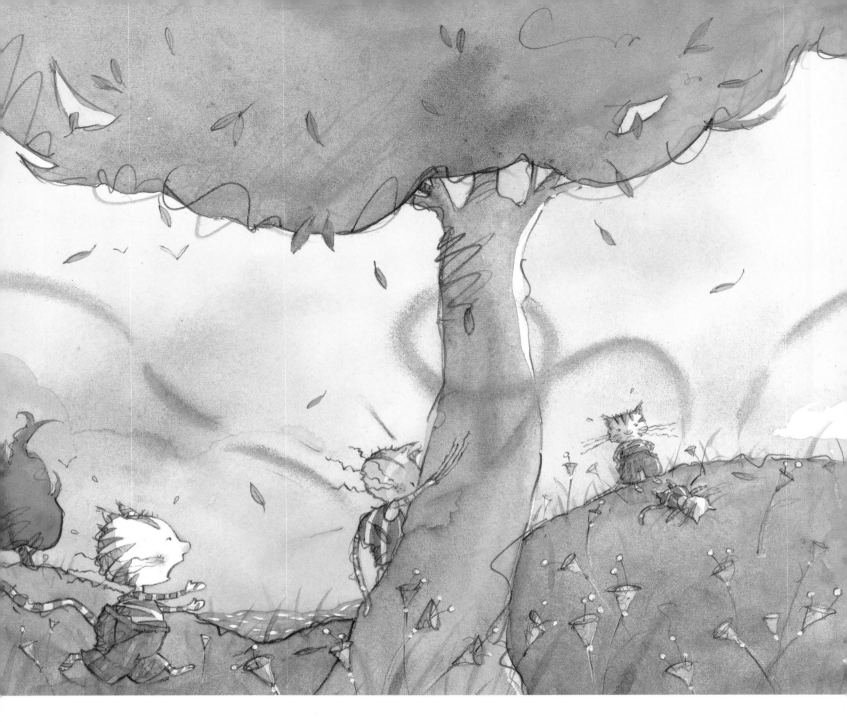

Caramba put on his earplugs and said, "Let's go for a walk, Henry."
Walking with Henry was exhausting. He didn't walk. He bumped into trees.
He fell flat on his face. He tangled himself up in clotheslines, kites and scarves.

Caramba ran this way and that.
Picking Henry up. Untangling Henry. Dusting Henry off.
There had to be another way.

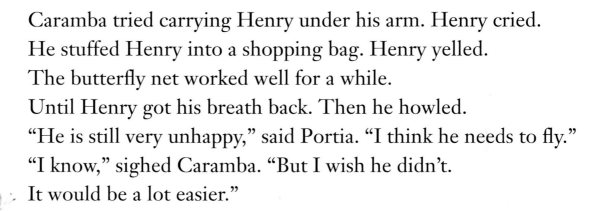

Caramba tried carrying Henry under his arm. Henry cried.

He stuffed Henry into a shopping bag. Henry yelled.

The butterfly net worked well for a while.

Until Henry got his breath back. Then he howled.

"He is still very unhappy," said Portia. "I think he needs to fly."

"I know," sighed Caramba. "But I wish he didn't.

It would be a lot easier."

Finally, Caramba had an idea.

"You're brilliant, Caramba!" giggled Portia. "Henry looks like a furry balloon."

Henry didn't like being laughed at. He didn't like Caramba's brilliant idea.

He wiggled and squirmed like a fish on a line.

"Stop pulling, Henry," said Caramba. "My arm is getting tired."

But Henry wriggled free. He disappeared into the darkening sky.

"Oh nooo!" cried Caramba. "What am I going to do?"

He splashed into the marsh and sank up to his waist in mud.

Portia pulled him out by the tail.

"We have to find Henry," she said.

"How?" asked Caramba. "I can't fly after him, and I can't swim in this muddy marsh."

"There's an old raft around here somewhere," said Portia. "Come on, Caramba! There's no time to lose."

Off they went in a cloud of dragonflies.

Frogs croaked.

Egrets stared at them from the corners of their yellow eyes.

"Have you seen a small cat flying by?" Caramba asked.

They shook their heads.

"The moon is rising," whispered Portia. "Now we can see where we are going."
"We're going nowhere," sighed Caramba. "We're going in circles."
Just then a scream rang out over the marsh. The frogs stopped croaking.

"That's Henry!" cried Caramba. "I'd recognize that scream anywhere."
He grabbed the pole and started pushing with all his might.
"Over there!" Portia yelled. She pointed to a tall tree towering over the marsh.

Henry was clinging to a small branch at the very top of the tree.
He was so scared he couldn't move.
"Henry!" cried Caramba. "I'm here!"
Henry *hoooowled*!
"Ssssh!" said Caramba. "Listen to me, Henry."

Henry stopped howling.
The frogs started croaking again. Owls hooted.
Bats *swiiiished* as they flitted by.
"Fly down, Henry," Caramba called softly. "Flap your arms!
Whirl your tail! I know you can do it."
Caramba opened his arms wide.

Henry took a deep breath.
He let go of the branch.
He flapped his arms slowly. Then faster.

He whirled his tail like a tiny egg-beater.
He flew down through the stars…
into Caramba's arms.

"Henry," said Caramba, "you fly so well. I am very proud of you."

"Car-r-r-amba," purred Henry.

It was Henry's first word.